W9-ASB-845

CONTENTS

LAKE CLASSICS

Great British and Irish
Short Stories I

SAKI

Stories retold by Joanne Suter
Illustrated by James McConnell

LAKE EDUCATION
Belmont, California

LAKE CLASSICS

Great American Short Stories I

Washington Irving, Nathaniel Hawthorne, Mark Twain, Bret Harte, Edgar Allan Poe, Kate Chopin, Willa Cather, Sarah Orne Jewett, Sherwood Anderson, Charles W. Chesnutt

Great American Short Stories II

Herman Melville, Stephen Crane, Ambrose Bierce, Jack London, Edith Wharton, Charlotte Perkins Gilman, Frank R. Stockton, Hamlin Garland, O. Henry, Richard Harding Davis

Great British and Irish Short Stories I

Arthur Conan Doyle, Saki (H. H. Munro), Rudyard Kipling, Katherine Mansfield, Thomas Hardy, E. M. Forster, Robert Louis Stevenson, H. G. Wells, John Galsworthy, James Joyce

Great Short Stories from Around the World I

Guy de Maupassant, Anton Chekhov, Leo Tolstoy, Selma Lagerlöf, Alphonse Daudet, Mori Ogwai, Leopoldo Alas, Rabindranath Tagore, Fyodor Dostoevsky, Honoré de Balzac

Cover and Text Designer: Diann Abbott

Copyright © 1994 by Lake Education, a division of Lake Publishing Company, 500 Harbor Blvd., Belmont, CA 94002. All rights reserved. No part of this book may be reproduced by any means, transmitted, or translated into a machine language without written permission from the publisher.

Library of Congress Catalog Number: 94-075352
ISBN 1-56103-027-9
Printed in the United States of America
1 9 8 7 6 5 4 3 2

❧ Lake Classic Short Stories ❧

"The universe is made of stories, not atoms."
—Muriel Rukeyser

"The story's about you."
—Horace

Everyone loves a good story. It is hard to think of a friendlier introduction to classic literature. For one thing, short stories are *short*—quick to get into and easy to finish. Of all the literary forms, the short story is the least intimidating and the most approachable.

Great literature is an important part of our human heritage. In the belief that this heritage belongs to everyone, *Lake Classic Short Stories* are adapted for today's readers. Lengthy sentences and paragraphs are shortened. Archaic words are replaced. Modern punctuation and spellings are used. Many of the longer stories are abridged. In all the stories, painstaking care has been taken to preserve the author's unique voice.

Lake Classic Short Stories have something for everyone. The hundreds of stories in the collection cover a broad terrain of themes, story types, and styles. Literary merit was a deciding factor in story selection. But no story was included unless it was as enjoyable as it was instructive. And special priority was given to stories that shine light on the human condition.

Each book in the *Lake Classic Short Stories* is devoted to the work of a single author. Little-known stories of merit are included with famous old favorites. Taken as a whole, the collected authors and stories make up a rich and diverse sampler of the story-teller's art.

Lake Classic Short Stories guarantee a great reading experience. Readers who look for common interests, concerns, and experiences are sure to find them. Readers who bring their own gifts of perception and appreciation to the stories will be doubly rewarded.

❦ Saki ❧
(1870–1916)

About the Author

Hector Hugh Munro was born a Scot in Burma. Not long after his birth, his parents sent him to England to be brought up by two strict old aunts. Apparently this was a miserable time for the boy. A child's resentment of his guardian is a recurring theme in his work.

In his early twenties, Munro went back to India. He took a job in Burma with the military police. But after only 13 months, he became so ill that he had to return to England.

Soon he became strong enough to begin his writing career. Under the pen name *Saki*, he wrote a series of political sketches which were published in a newspaper. Later, he worked as a foreign correspondent in Russia and in the

Balkans. There he wrote many of the humorous stories for which he is remembered. He also wrote two novels, three plays, and one book of history.

In one series of humorous short stories, Saki created two popular characters—Reginald and Clovis. These two young men spend their time taking light-hearted revenge on the adult world. Other stories, such as *Sredni Vashtar*, are truly grim and gruesome.

Saki was 44 years old when he volunteered for service during World War I. He entered the military as a private, even though he was offered an officer's rank. At the age of 46, he was sent to the battlefields of France as a corporal. In November 1916, he was killed in action.

Some of Saki's stories are very funny. Others have a strange, eerie quality. But all of his tales are entertaining. As you read the following stories, look for both the humor and the weirdness. You won't be disappointed.

Sredni Vashtar

Have you ever longed for revenge? In this famous story, a mean, thoughtless guardian makes a boy's life miserable. What chance does a sickly child have against a powerful adult? Not much—unless he gets a little outside help.

IN THE SUMMER, CONRADIN LAID RED FLOWERS BEFORE
THE SHRINE OF SREDNI VASHTAR.

Sredni Vashtar

Conradin was ten years old. In the doctor's judgment, the boy would not live another five years. In Conradin's judgment, the doctor was a weak, tired man and counted for little. But his opinion was backed up by Mrs. De Ropp, who counted for nearly everything. Mrs. De Ropp was Conradin's cousin and guardian. In Conradin's eyes she stood for the parts of the world that are necessary and disagreeable and real.

The rest of Conradin's world was made up of himself and his imagination. One of these days Conradin supposed he would have to give in to the world of illnesses and rules. He would die of boredom. Without his imagination, which was fed by loneliness, he would have given in long ago.

Mrs. De Ropp would never have admitted to herself that she did not like Conradin. Yet, spoiling his fun "for his own good" was a job she did not mind at all. Conradin hated her deeply, but he was perfectly able to hide that hatred. The boy had few joys in life. Causing trouble for Mrs. De Ropp was his greatest happiness. From the secret world of his imagination, she was locked out. She was an unclean thing that could never enter there.

Conradin found little fun in the dull, cheerless garden that circled the house. Windows were always likely to open and a scolding shouted out not to do this or that. Mrs. De Ropp would call out that medicines were due. He was not allowed to touch the few fruits that grew on the spindly trees.

But in one forgotten corner of the

garden there stood an old tool shed. It was almost hidden behind a large, dark bush. Within the walls of the tool shed, Conradin made his own special place. It became both his playroom and his church. He had peopled it with imaginary friends, made up partly from stories and partly from his own brain.

But the tool shed also had two residents of flesh and blood. In one corner lived a black and white hen. Because he had little else to care for, Conradin truly loved the ragged-feathered hen. Farther back in the dark stood a large hutch. It was fronted with iron bars. The hutch was the home of a large polecat-ferret. Conradin had saved bits of silver until he could buy the ferret. A friendly butcher-boy had sneaked it—cage and all—into the old tool shed. Conradin was dreadfully afraid of the sharp-fanged beast. But it meant more to him than anything he owned. Its vary presence in the tool shed was a fearful joy. It was a secret to be kept from The Woman, as he privately named her.

One day Conradin thought of a wonderful name for the beast. From that moment, the animal somehow grew into a god and a religion. Conradin made up his own special ceremonies. Every Thursday, he went to the dark and dusty silence of the tool shed. There he worshipped before the wooden hutch of Sredni Vashtar, the great ferret. In the summer, Conradin laid red flowers before the shrine of Sredni Vashtar. In the winter, he carried in sprigs of red berries. And on great holidays powdered nutmeg was sprinkled in front of his hutch. Of course, the nutmeg had to be stolen from The Woman.

There were not many of these holidays, but each marked some wonderful event that delighted Conradin. One time, Mrs. De Ropp had a terrible toothache for three days. Conradin continued the holiday for the whole three days. He did, in fact, almost come to believe that Sredni Vashtar had caused that terrible toothache. If the pain had lasted for another day, the supply of nutmeg would have given out.

One day Mrs. De Ropp began to notice Conradin's interest in the tool shed. "It is not good for him to be wasting time down there in all weathers," she quickly decided.

At breakfast the next morning she announced that the black and white hen had been sold and taken away overnight. With her short-sighted eyes she peered at Conradin. She waited for his cries of rage or sorrow. As ever, she was ready to scold him about good behavior. But Conradin said nothing. There was nothing to be said. Something in the set look on his white face made her feel a bit uneasy.

At tea that afternoon there was toast on the table. Mrs. De Ropp almost never made toast for Conradin. She said it was bad for him. Also, the making of it "gave trouble"—a deadly sin in Mrs. De Ropp's opinion.

Conradin did not touch the treat. "I thought you liked toast," Mrs. De Ropp exclaimed in a hurt tone.

"Sometimes," said Conradin.

In the shed that evening something new was added to the worship of the hutch-god. Conradin usually chanted the ferret's praises. Tonight he asked a favor.

"Do one thing for me, Sredni Vashtar."

The thing was not described. Since Sredni Vashtar was a god, he would know. Conradin held back a sob as he looked at the other empty corner of the shed. How he missed the black and white hen! Then he went back to the world he so hated.

Every night Conradin knelt in the welcome darkness of his bedroom. And every evening he knelt in the dusty tool shed. In each place, Conradin prayed bitterly, "Do one thing for me, Sredni Vashtar."

Mrs. De Ropp noticed that the visits to the shed did not stop. One day she decided to see what was going on.

"What are you keeping in that locked hutch?" she asked. "I believe it's guinea pigs. I'll have them all cleared away."

Conradin shut his lips tight. The

Woman searched through his bedroom until she found the carefully hidden key. Then she marched right down to the tool shed.

It was a cold afternoon. Conradin had been told to keep to the house. From the furthest window of the dining room, the door of the shed could just be seen. Conradin stood silently at that window. He saw The Woman enter the shed. He imagined her opening the door of the sacred hutch. He pictured her peeking in with her short-sighted eyes. He imagined her poking a stick into the thick straw bed where his god lay hidden. With great feeling, Conradin breathed his prayer for the last time: "Do one thing for me, Sredni Vashtar."

But he knew as he prayed that he did not believe. He knew that The Woman would soon come out of the shed. He could picture that tight little smile that he hated upon her face. He was sure that in an hour or two the gardener would carry away his wonderful god. But then it would be a god no longer, but only a simple brown ferret in a hutch. Somehow he knew that The Woman would win over him always—as she won now. He would grow ever more sickly under her rules and scoldings. Finally the day would come when nothing would matter to him anymore. The doctor would be proved right. And in the sting and sorrow of his defeat, he began to chant loudly. He chanted the song of Sredni Vashtar:

Sredni Vashtar went forth,
His thoughts were red thoughts and his
*   teeth were white.*
His enemies called for peace, but he
*   brought them death.*
Sredni Vashtar the Beautiful.

And then, all of a sudden, he stopped his chanting. He moved closer to the window. The door of the shed was still open, and the minutes were slipping by. He watched little birds running and flying across the lawn. He counted them over and over again. But he kept one eye always on that swinging door. After a while a sour-faced maid came in to lay the table for tea. Still Conradin stood and waited and watched. Hope had crept by inches into his heart. And now a look of triumph began to burn in his eyes. Under his breath he began a chant of victory. Before long his hopes were rewarded.

Out through the door of the shed came a long, low, yellow and brown beast. Its eyes blinked at the fading daylight. There were dark wet stains around the fur of the animal's jaws and throat. Conradin dropped to his knees. The great polecat-ferret made its way down to a small brook at the foot of the garden. It drank for a moment. Then it crossed a little wooden bridge and was lost to sight in the bushes. Such was the passing of Sredni Vashtar.

"Tea is ready," said the sour-faced maid. "Where is the mistress?"

"She went down to the shed some time ago," said Conradin.

And while the maid went to call her mistress to tea, Conradin fished a toasting-fork out of a drawer. He began to toast himself a piece of bread. Then he smeared it with much butter. As he slowly ate the toast, Conradin listened to the noises and silences beyond the dining room door.

First there was the long, silly screaming of the maid. Then came the answering cries from the kitchen. There were quick footsteps and hurried calls for outside help. Then, after a moment of quiet, came the scared sobbings and the shuffling steps of those who bore a heavy burden into the house.

"Whoever will break it to the poor child? I couldn't for the life of me!" exclaimed a high voice. And while they talked over the matter among themselves, Conradin made himself another piece of toast.

The Open Window

Do you feel comfortable meeting new people? Well, Framton Nuttel doesn't. In this story, a nervous young man visits the country to "rest his nerves." What he finds there is anything but restful.

"OUT THAT WINDOW, THREE YEARS AGO TO THIS DAY,
MY AUNT'S HUSBAND WENT OFF FOR A DAY'S HUNTING."

The Open
Window

"My aunt will be down in a moment, Mr. Nuttel," said the smiling young lady. She seemed very sure of herself for only 15. "In the meantime, you must try and put up with me."

Framton Nuttel tried to say something that would charm the girl while he waited for her aunt. In his heart he was not sure exactly what he was doing in this strange house. Framton was a very nervous man. He had come to the country to rest and relax.

"You must make an effort to meet people," his sister had said when he was planning his trip. "I'm afraid you will keep to yourself down there and not speak to a living soul. Your nerves will be worse than ever if you sit around alone. I shall give you letters that will introduce you to all the people I know there. As I remember, some of them were quite nice."

Now Framton Nuttel wondered about Mrs. Sappleton. The girl's aunt was a stranger to him, of course. He would soon be giving her one of the letters. Would she be among the "nice" people?

The silence in the room had grown uncomfortable. "Do you know many of the people around here?" asked the niece.

"Hardly a soul," said Framton. "My sister spent some time here about four years ago. She gave me letters of introduction to a few of the people she had met."

He sounded as if he were a bit sorry he had come.

"Then you know almost nothing about my aunt?" asked the young lady.

"Only her name and her address,"

answered Framton. He was wondering whether Mrs. Sappleton was a married woman or a widow. Something about the room suggested that a man lived there.

"Her great tragedy happened just three years ago," said the girl. "That would be since your sister was here."

"Her tragedy?" asked Framton in alarm. Somehow tragedies seemed out of place in the restful countryside.

"You may wonder why we keep that window wide open on an October afternoon," said the niece. She pointed to a large French window that opened as a door onto the lawn.

"It is quite warm for the time of year," said Framton. "But has that window got anything to do with the tragedy?"

"Out through that window, three years ago to this day, my aunt's husband went off for a day's hunting. Her two young brothers went along with him. They never came back! In crossing the moor to their favorite hunting ground they all disappeared. It seems that all three were swallowed up by a dangerous swamp.

That summer was dreadfully wet, you know. Places that were safe in other years suddenly gave way without warning. Their bodies were never found. That was the dreadful part of it."

Here the girl's voice lost its calm note and became unsteady. "Poor aunt always thinks that they will come back some day. She imagines that they will return with the little brown dog that was lost with them. She expects them to walk in through that window just as they used to do! That is why the window is kept open every evening until it is quite dark.

"Poor dear aunt has often told me how they went out. There was her husband, carrying his white raincoat over his arm. With him was Ronnie, her youngest brother. Ronnie was singing 'Bertie, Why Do you Bound?' as he always liked to do to tease her.

"He knew how that silly song got on her nerves. That was the last time anybody ever saw them. Do you know something strange? Sometimes on quiet evenings like this, I get a creepy feeling that they *will* walk in through that window. . . ."

She shivered just a little as her words broke off. Framton was glad when the aunt suddenly entered the room.

"So sorry I kept you waiting," she said. "I trust that Vera has been keeping you good company?"

"She has been very interesting," said Framton.

"I hope you don't mind the open window," said Mrs. Sappleton. "My husband and brothers will be home any moment from shooting. They always come in this way. Today they have been out hunting birds in the marshes. No doubt, they'll make a fine mess over my poor carpets! So like you men, isn't it?"

She talked on cheerfully about the shooting and the lack of birds this season. To Framton it was all just horrible. He tried to turn the talk to a less frightening topic. He saw that Mrs. Sappleton's eyes often glanced at the open window and the lawn beyond. The anniversary of the tragedy was certainly the wrong day to pay his visit!

"My doctors agree I need complete rest," Framton announced. "I'm supposed to stay away from any excitement, they say, or any hard physical exercise." For some reason, he always thought that total strangers were interested in his illnesses, their cause and cure. "As to what I should and should not eat," he went on, "they cannot seem to agree."

"No?" said Mrs. Sappleton. She put her hand over her mouth to hide a yawn. Then she brightened. Something other than Framton's words had caught her attention.

"Here they are at last!" she cried. "Just in time for tea. And don't they look as if they are muddy up to the eyes!"

Framton shivered slightly. He turned towards the niece with a look that said he understood her poor aunt's problems. But the girl was staring out through the open window with dazed horror in her eyes. In a chill shock of nameless fear Framton swung around in his seat. He looked in the same direction.

In the deepening evening light, three figures were walking across the lawn. They were moving towards the window. All of them carried guns under their arms. One had a white coat hung over his shoulders. A tired brown dog kept close at their heels. Silently they came closer and closer to the house. Then a young voice sang out of the dusk: "I said, Bertie, why do you bound?"

Framton grabbed wildly at his hat. He barely saw the hall door, the driveway, or the front gate as he escaped. A fellow on a bicycle almost ran into the hedge to avoid crashing into him.

"Here we are, my dear," said the man with the white raincoat as he came in through the window. "Our boots are fairly muddy, I'm afraid. But most of it is dry. Who was that man running out as we came up?"

"A very unusual fellow, a Mr. Nuttel," said Mrs. Sappleton. "He could only talk about all of his illnesses. Then, when you three arrived, he dashed off without even a word of good-bye! One would think that he had seen a ghost."

"I expect it was the dog," said the niece calmly. "He told me he was deathly afraid of dogs. Ever since he was hunted into a cemetery by a pack of wild dogs. The poor man had to spend the night in a newly dug grave. All night, the beasts were snapping and grinning and foaming at the mouth just above him. It would be enough to make anyone lose his nerve!"

Spinning such tales at short notice was her specialty.

Tobermory

Some people would give anything to know what their pets are thinking. In this hilarious story, an animal trainer shows off his best student. Why aren't Mrs. Blemley's houseguests clapping and cheering?

THE MAJOR WAS NOT THE ONLY ONE TO FEEL PANIC.
THE GUESTS WERE NOW LOOKING VERY UNHAPPY.

Tobermory

Lady Blemley was having a house party. It was a cool, rain-washed afternoon. In August, there was nothing much to hunt and nothing much to do. But just now, her guests were happily gathered around the tea table. Their open-mouthed attention was fixed on one person.

In looks, Mr. Cornelius Appin was rather homely and uninteresting. No one knew anything about him. Even Lady Blemley didn't know him very well. But someone had told her that Mr. Appin was "clever." She had invited him in the hope that some of his cleverness might entertain her guests.

Until tea-time that day she had been unable to discover any cleverness at all. He had not been skillful at either sports or conversation. And he was not so charming that women were willing to forgive his lack of wit. He had faded into nothing but plain old Mr. Appin. Even the name Cornelius seemed too fancy for him.

But now he was saying that he had given the world a wonderful discovery. Alongside of his discovery, the inventions of gunpowder and the printing press were mere nothings. Of course science had made giant leaps during recent years. But what he was talking about seemed to be more of a miracle rather than a scientific discovery.

"How can you ask us to believe this?" Sir Wilfrid Blemley laughed. "You say that you have discovered a way to teach animals to talk? And you say that our cat Tobermory has become your first successful pupil?"

"I have worked on this project for the last 17 years," said Mr. Appin with a smile. "But only during the last eight or nine months have I had some success. Of course I have experimented with thousands of animals. But only recently have I worked with cats, those wonderful creatures.

"Just think of it. They live so quietly in our homes—yet keep all their highly developed wild instincts! Here and there among cats one comes across a top mind, just as one does among human beings. When I met Tobermory a week ago, I saw at once that I had found the smartest cat. I had already made good progress along the road to success. But with Tobermory, as you call him, I have reached the goal."

Mr. Appin tried not to sound too proud of himself as he ended his surprising statement. No one said "Rats!" aloud. But a man named Clovis moved his lips a bit to form that word of disbelief.

After a moment, Miss Resker spoke. "Do you mean to say that you have taught Tobermory to say and understand certain words and easy, short sentences?"

"My dear Miss Resker," smiled the wonder-worker Appin. "Little children are taught in that way. When one is working with such a fine mind—even in an animal—one has no need for such simple ways. Tobermory can speak our language perfectly."

This time Clovis very clearly said, "Beyond-rats!" Sir Wilfrid was more polite, but equally unbelieving.

"Hadn't we better have the cat in and see for ourselves?" asked Lady Blemley.

Sir Wilfrid went to look for the animal. The company settled themselves down. They were ready to see Mr. Appin do a magic trick or throw his voice.

In a minute Sir Wilfrid was back in the room. His face was white under its tan. His eyes were wide.

"By Gad, it's true!"

His excitement was very real. The others leaned forward. Their interest was awakened.

Falling into a chair, Sir Wilfrid gasped: "I found Tobermory resting in the drawing room. I called out to him to come in for his tea. He just blinked at me in his usual way. Then I said, 'Come on, Toby. Don't keep us waiting.' Then, by Gad, he answered me in a most horribly human voice. He said he'd come when he good and well pleased! I nearly jumped out of my skin!"

When Appin had told his story, no one believed him. But Sir Wilfrid's words were instantly accepted as being true. Everyone started talking at once. The scientist Appin sat silently. He was very much enjoying the first glory of his wonderful success.

In the midst of the noise, Tobermory entered the room. He made his way with soft steps. His face showed a definite lack of interest in the group seated around the tea table.

A sudden quiet fell on the company. They seemed too embarrassed to speak on even terms with a talking house cat.

"Will you have some milk, Tobermory?" asked Lady Blemley in a rather tight voice. She looked at the cat uncertainly.

"I don't mind if I do," was the answer. His voice sounded rather bored. A shiver of excitement went through the guests. It was no wonder that Lady Blemley shook as she poured the dish of milk.

"I'm afraid I've spilt a good deal of it," she said.

"No matter. It's not my carpet," was Tobermory's reply.

Another silence fell on the group. Then Miss Resker, in her best manner, asked the cat a question. She wanted to know if the human language had been hard to learn. Tobermory looked straight at her for a moment. Then he turned his eyes away. It appeared that he found her question quite boring.

"What do you think of human intelligence?" asked Mavis Pellington weakly.

"Of whose intelligence in particular?" asked Tobermory coldly.

"Oh, well, mine for instance," said Mavis with a tiny laugh.

"You put me in an embarrassing spot," said Tobermory.

But his proud manner certainly did not suggest a bit of embarrassment. "I remember hearing your name when the guest list for this house party was discussed. Sir Wilfrid said that you were the most brainless woman he had ever known. Lady Blemley replied that your lack of brain-power was just what got you invited. It seems you were the only person she could think of who might be stupid enough to buy their old car. You know—the one that goes quite nicely uphill if you push it."

Lady Blemley tried to deny it all. But just that morning she had told Mavis about the car. She had said that it would be just the thing for Mavis's country home.

Major Barfield broke in to change the subject. He decided to talk to Tobermory man-to-man.

"How about your carryings-on with the little brown tabby-cat up at the stables, eh, old boy?"

The moment he said it, everyone realized the mistake.

"One does not usually discuss such matters among mixed company," said Tobermory coldly. "I've noted your ways since you've been in this house. I should imagine that you'd find it rather uncomfortable if I were to turn the talk to your *own* little affairs."

The Major was not the only one to panic after that statement. The guests were now looking very unhappy.

"Would you like to go and see if the cook has got your dinner ready?" asked Lady Blemley quickly. No matter that it was at least two hours until Tobermory's dinner time.

"Thanks," said Tobermory. "But not quite so soon after my tea. I don't want to die of overeating."

"Cats have nine lives, you know," said Sir Wilfrid heartily.

"Possibly," answered Tobermory, "but only one liver."

"Adelaide Blemley!" said Mrs. Cornett, "do you mean to allow that cat to go out and talk about us in the servants' hall?"

By now the guests had all panicked.

They were thinking about the narrow ledge that ran in front of the bedroom windows at Lady Blemley's. It was remembered that this had been a favorite walkway for Tobermory at all hours. The guests were worried. From that ledge Tobermory could have been watching the birds—or heaven knew what else! What if he planned to tell all he had seen? The effect on many of the guests could be more than a little upsetting.

Mrs. Cornett was a woman who spent much time before her mirror and owed her looks to make-up. The idea of the cat talking made her as ill at ease as the Major.

Miss Scrawen, who wrote love poems but in truth lived a lonely life, looked unhappy too. After all, if you have no excitement in your private life, you would rather not have everyone know about it.

Bertie van Tahn had been getting into trouble ever since he was 17. The possible telling of his secrets turned his face a dull, pasty shade of white.

Clovis was able to remain calm on the outside. But in his head he was busy wondering where he could buy a box of fancy mice. That might be one way to buy Tobermory's silence.

Even in all the excitement, Agnes Resker could not stand being in the background for too long.

"Why did I ever come down here?" she asked with great show.

Tobermory quickly took the opening.

"Judging by what you said to Mrs. Cornett on the croquet lawn yesterday, you were out for the food. You said the Blemleys were the dullest people you knew. But they were clever enough, you said, to have a first-rate cook. Otherwise they'd find it hard to get any guests to come back a second time."

"There's not a word of truth in it!" Agnes howled. "Just ask Mrs. Cornett!"

"Mrs. Cornett repeated your words later to Bertie van Tahn," he went on. "'That woman is a regular pig. She'd go anywhere for four square meals a day,'

is what she said. Then Bertie van Tahn
said . . . ”

Luckily for Agnes, at this point the
story stopped. Tobermory had caught
sight of the big yellow tomcat from the
parson's cottage. The huge cat was
working his way through the bushes
towards the stables. In a flash Tobermory
had disappeared through the open
French window.

With the disappearance of his too-
clever pupil, Cornelius Appin found
himself under attack. The guests set
upon the poor man a storm of scoldings
and worried questions. The whole mess
was all his fault! He must stop matters
from becoming worse!

Could Tobermory share his dangerous
gift with other cats? This was the
question that most frightened them. It
was possible, Appin replied. Yes, he
might have shared his talent with his
close friend, the stable tabby-cat. But it
was not likely that his teaching could
have spread much farther as yet.

“That settles it,” said Mrs. Cornett,

"I'm sure you'll agree with me, Adelaide. Tobermory may be a valuable cat and a great pet. But both he and the stable cat must be done away with. And the sooner the better."

"You don't suppose I've enjoyed the last quarter of an hour, do you?" Lady Blemley asked bitterly. "My husband and I are very fond of Tobermory. At least, we *were* before this horrible talent was given to him. But now, of course, there is only one thing to do. We must have him destroyed as soon as possible."

"Perhaps we can put some poison in the scraps he always gets at dinner time," said Sir Wilfrid. "And I will go and drown the stable cat myself. The stable man will be very angry at losing his pet. But I will say both cats fell sick and we're afraid of it spreading to the kennels."

"But what about my great discovery?" cried Mr. Appin. "After all my years of work . . ."

"You can go and work with the sheep at the farm. They, at least, are under proper control," said Mrs. Cornett. "Or

work with the elephants at the zoo.
They're said to be very smart. Best of all,
they don't come crawling about our
bedrooms and under chairs and so forth."

Cornelius Appin was heart-broken.
The response to his wonderful discovery
left him speechless. But the group was
set against him. In fact, if a vote had
been taken, they might have wanted to
give him poison, too.

The guests stayed on, for everyone
hoped to see matters brought to a finish.
But dinner that evening went rather
badly. Sir Wilfrid had had a hard time
with the stable cat and also with the
stable man. Agnes Resker made a great
show of being upset. She ate only a tiny
bite of dry toast which she bit into as
though it were her enemy. Mavis
Pellington kept coldly silent throughout
the meal.

Lady Blemley kept up the flow of talk,
but her eyes stayed on the doorway. A
plate full of carefully poisoned fish scraps
was waiting on the sideboard. Dinner
and dessert came and then went. Yet

Tobermory did not appear either in the dining room or kitchen.

The deathly chill of dinner was cheerful compared to the following hours in the parlor. Eating and drinking had at least been something to do. The guests could hide their embarrassment as long as they were busy. Yet now a game of cards was out of the question. Everyone was either too nervous or too angry. Odo Finsberry sang a silly song. That put an end to any thought of more music.

At 11:00 the servants went to bed. They announced that the pantry had been left open as usual for Tobermory's use. Hour after hour, the guests read magazines as Lady Blemley made visits to the pantry. Each time she returned with a sad, disappointed look, shaking her head slowly.

At 2:00 in the morning, Clovis broke the heavy silence.

"He won't turn up tonight. He's probably in the town newspaper office right now, telling everything he knows. It will be the news story of the day!"

Having added those words to the general air of cheerfulness, Clovis went to bed. Slowly, the other members of the house party followed his lead.

The next morning the servants took around early tea. They heard the same question in each room, and they gave the same answer: Tobermory had not returned.

Breakfast was, if anything, even more unpleasant than dinner had been. But before the meal ended, the problem was solved. Tobermory's body was brought in from the bushes, where a gardener had just discovered it. There were bites on his neck. Yellow fur coated his claws. It was clear that he had been in battle with the big tomcat from the parson's cottage.

By afternoon most of the guests had left the Blemleys' home. After lunch, Lady Blemley felt well enough to write a very ugly letter to the parson about the loss of her valuable pet.

Tobermory had been Appin's one successful pupil. He would have no others. A few weeks later an elephant in the zoo, which had never before caused problems, broke loose. It killed an Englishman who had been teasing it. The dead man's name was reported in different papers as Oppin and Eppelin. His first name, however, was correctly listed as Cornelius.

"If he was finding fault with the animal's grammar," said Clovis, "he deserved all he got."

Dusk

Does everyone who asks
deserve your help? Some
hard-luck stories are hard
to believe. In this amusing
story, Norman Gortsby has
to make a decision. Is the
man on the park bench
telling him the truth?

MEN AND WOMEN WHO HAD FOUGHT AND LOST CAME
FORTH IN THIS HOUR OF FADING LIGHT.

Dusk

Norman Gortsby sat on a bench in the park. To his back was a strip of bushes fenced by railings. Before him, just past a wide drive, stood a row of tall houses. Hyde Park Corner, with its rattle and hoot of traffic, lay just to his right.

It was about 6:30 on an early March evening. Dusk had fallen heavily over the scene. The deepening darkness was softened by some faint moonlight and many street lamps. Somehow the road and sidewalk had an empty feeling, even though there were people about. They could hardly be seen as they moved silently through the half light or sat quietly on benches. It was hard to separate these figures from the shadowed gloom in which they sat.

The scene pleased Gortsby. It matched his present mood. Dusk, to his mind, was the hour of the defeated. Men and women who had fought and lost came forth in this hour of fading light. There they hid their bad luck and dead hopes from the eyes of others. In the dusk, their shabby clothes and bowed shoulders and unhappy eyes might pass without notice.

A king that is conquered must see strange looks,
So bitter a thing is the heart of man.

Those who wandered in the dusk did not choose to have strange looks fasten on them. So they came out at dusk, like bats. They came to the park when it had been emptied of laughing people and playing children.

Brightly lit windows glowed in the dusk. They marked the homes of those other people who were winners in life's struggle. Or at least those who had not yet had to admit their failures.

These were Gortsby's thoughts as he sat on his bench on the lonely path. He was in the mood to count himself among the defeated. It was not as if he had money troubles. If he had so wished, he could have walked into the streets of light and noise. He could have taken his place among those who had jobs and money. Gortsby had failed in other ways. But at that moment he was heart-sore and unhappy. This evening he felt more like those who wandered in the dark stretches between the lamp lights.

On the bench by his side sat an old gentleman. The old fellow looked like he might have once been somebody of importance. His clothes were not exactly shabby, but he was not well-dressed either. It was hard to imagine him with enough money to buy a fine box of chocolates or a flower for his lapel. He looked miserable, like a member of some forgotten band to whose music no one dances. Clearly, the old man was one of the world's sad and lonely people for whom no one cries.

As the man rose to leave, Gortsby imagined the home to which he was returning. No doubt he got little attention there and was held of no account. Or perhaps he was headed for some cheerless lodging where paying a weekly bill was all that concerned him. His figure disappeared slowly into the shadows.

Right away the old gentleman's place on the bench was taken by a young man. He was fairly well dressed but seemed just as sad as the old fellow before him. As if to say the world went badly with him, the newcomer swore angrily and out loud. He flung himself down on the bench.

It seemed to Gortsby that he was expected to take notice of the show. "You don't seem to be in a very good temper," he said.

The young man turned to look at him. "You wouldn't be in a good temper either if you were in the fix I'm in," he said. "I've done the silliest thing I've ever done in my life."

"Yes?" said Gortsby politely.

"I came to London this afternoon, meaning to stay at a certain hotel in Berkshire Square," continued the young man. "When I got there, I found it had been torn down some weeks ago. A movie theater was going up on the spot. The taxi driver suggested another hotel some way off, so I went there. The first thing I did was to send a letter to my family giving them the address. Then I went out to buy some soap. I'd forgotten to pack any, you see, and I hate using hotel soap. After I bought the soap, I strolled about a bit. I had a cup of coffee and looked at the shops. Then I turned back to the hotel. But all of a sudden I realized that I didn't remember the name of the place or even what street it was on. There's a nice mess for a fellow who has no friends in London!

"Of course I can wire my family for the address, but they won't have gotten my

letter until tomorrow. For now, I'm
without any money. I went out with just
enough to buy the soap and get a coffee.
Now here I am, wandering about with
next to nothing in my pocket and
nowhere to go for the night."

There was a long pause after the story
had been told. "I suppose my story is
rather hard to believe," said the young
man at last. There was just a hint of
anger in his voice.

"Not at all," said Gortsby. "I remember
doing exactly the same thing once in a
foreign capital. Only there were two of
us, which made it even more unlikely.
Luckily we remembered that the hotel
was on a sort of canal. When we finally
came to the canal, we were able to find
our way back to the hotel."

The youth brightened at Gortsby's
story. "In a foreign city I wouldn't mind
so much," he said. "I could go to the
embassy and get help. In one's own land,
it's a much bigger problem. Unless I can
find some kindly fellow to believe my
story and lend me some money, I seem

likely to spend the night outdoors. I'm glad, anyhow, that you don't think my story is totally impossible."

He threw a good deal of warmth into his last words. It was as though he hoped that Gortsby did not fall far short of the necessary kindness.

"Of course," said Gortsby slowly, "there is a weak point to your story. You don't have the soap."

The young man sat forward quickly. He felt in the pockets of his overcoat and then jumped to his feet.

"I must have lost it," he said angrily.

"To lose a hotel and a cake of soap in one afternoon seems very careless," said Gortsby. But the young man did not wait to hear the end of the remark. He stamped off down the path with his head held high.

"It was too bad," thought Gortsby aloud. "The going out to get one's own soap was the one believable touch in the whole story. And yet it was just that little bit that caused him a problem. He should have thought ahead to carry a cake of soap, wrapped and sealed carefully. Then he would have had a perfect tale. In tricking people, one must carefully watch the details."

With that thought, Gortsby rose to go. But as he did so, a cry escaped him. Lying on the ground by the side of the bench was a small, round package. It was carefully wrapped and sealed. What else could it be but a cake of soap! No doubt it had fallen out of the young man's overcoat pocket when he sat down on the bench.

In another moment Gortsby was running through the dusk. He hurried down the dark path in search of a young figure in a light overcoat. He had nearly given up the search when he caught sight of the man standing beside the drive. He seemed to be deciding whether to start out across the park or head for the busy sidewalks of Knightsbridge. The young man turned around sharply when he heard Gortsby call him.

"The proof of your story has turned up," said Gortsby. He held out the cake of soap. "It must have slipped out of your overcoat pocket when you sat down on the bench. I saw it on the ground after you left. I'm sorry I didn't believe you at first. But now that I see the cake of soap, I can only accept your story as true. If this small loan is any good to you . . ."

The young man quickly pocketed the money.

"Here is my card with my address," continued Gortsby. "Any day this week will do for returning the money. And here is the soap. Don't lose it again. It's been a good friend to you."

"Lucky thing your finding it," said the youth. With a catch in his voice, he said a word or two of thanks. Then he fled quickly in the direction of Knightsbridge.

"Poor boy, he nearly broke down," said Gortsby to himself. "I can easily see why. It must be a great relief to have his problem solved. It's a lesson to me not to judge others too quickly."

Gortsby walked back past the bench where he had first met the young man.

There he saw an older gentleman poking and peeking beneath the seat. The man searched the ground all around the bench. Gortsby saw it was the fellow who had been sitting on the bench earlier that evening.

"Have you lost anything, sir?" he asked.

"Yes, sir, a cake of soap."

The Mouse

Have you ever had an embarrassing moment? In this story, a prim and proper young man faces his worst nightmare. What will the woman on the train think of him?

SUDDENLY HE BECAME ALL TOO AWARE THAT HE WAS
NOT ALONE WITH THE SLEEPING YOUNG LADY.

The Mouse

Theodoric Voler had been brought up by a very careful mother who was full of worries and fears. From the time he was a baby until he reached middle age, her chief care had been to protect him. She made sure he didn't have to deal with what she called the rougher realities of life. When the old lady died, Theodoric was left alone in the world. And he found that world was a good deal rougher than he wished it were.

To a man of his nature and background, even a simple train journey was full of little problems and worries. As he settled himself down in a second-class car one September morning, he realized he was quite upset.

Theodoric had been staying at a country home where things had been less than orderly. The servant there had forgotten to call the pony carriage that was to take him to the train station. When it came time for him to leave, there was no carriage in sight. Theodoric was angry, but he hid his upset. He decided to be brave about it and harness the pony himself.

This meant he had to hunt for a harness in a smelly stable. In certain places, the stable had the distinct odor of mice. Theodoric was not actually afraid of mice. But he classed them among the rougher parts of life. He believed that God might have long ago seen that they were not needed—and removed them from the earth.

As the train left the station, Theodoric was sure that he, himself, smelled a bit like the stable. He worried that an old straw or two still clung to his usually well-brushed clothing. Fortunately there was only one other person riding in the train car. She was a lady of about his own age. Theodoric was glad that she seemed more interested in sleeping than in taking note of him.

The train was not due to stop until the end of the line, in about an hour's time. The cars were of the old-fashioned sort with no passageway connecting them. Therefore, no further travelers were likely to join the two.

And yet, the train had hardly left the station when Theodoric started feeling uneasy. Suddenly he became all too aware that he was not alone with the sleeping lady. He was not even alone in his own clothes. He felt a warm, creeping movement over his skin. Somehow an unseen but very active stray mouse had dashed into his clothes while Theodoric harnessed the pony. Secret foot-stamping and a few wild pinches did not shake the uninvited mouse loose.

Theodoric, the rightful wearer of the clothes, lay back against the seat. He frowned in thought, trying to come up with some way of ending the shared ownership of his suit. It was simply unthinkable that could continue for a whole hour as a hotel for homeless mice. (Already in his mind the number of uninvited guests had at least doubled.)

On the other hand, nothing less than partly undressing himself would get rid of the pest. And how could he undress in front of a lady, even for such a good reason? The very idea made his ears burn and turn bright red. He had never even been able to wear socks that showed his ankles in the presence of ladies. And yet, the lady in this case appeared to be soundly and safely asleep. The mouse, on the other hand, seemed to be busily taking a hike up his body.

Theodoric wondered if there were any truth to the idea that people, after death, return to earth as animals. If so, this particular mouse must certainly have been, in a former life, a member of a mountain-climbing club. Sometimes in its eagerness, the mouse lost its footing and slipped for half an inch or so. Then, in fright, or more probably in anger, it bit and scratched.

At last Theodoric was forced into the bravest undertaking of his life. He kept a careful watch on the sleeping lady. Then, turning as red as a beet, he moved swiftly and silently to solve his problem. He tied the ends of a traveling blanket to the racks on either side of the car. In that way he turned the blanket into a sturdy curtain. Hanging across the car, it separated him from his fellow traveler. In this narrow dressing-room, he hurriedly began to get himself partly, and the mouse entirely, out of his clothing.

The freed mouse gave a wild leap to the floor. But just as suddenly the blanket slipped its fastenings at both ends. It came down with a terrible flop. At that exact moment the awakened sleeper opened her eyes. With a movement almost quicker than the mouse's, Theodoric grabbed the blanket. He pulled it chin-high over himself. Then he dove into a seat in the farthest corner of the car. The blood raced in the veins of his neck and forehead. He was sure the young lady would scream and pull the emergency cord to stop the train. The lady, however, only stared silently at her strangely wrapped companion. How much had she seen, Theodoric wondered to himself. And what on earth must she think of him?

"I think I have caught a chill," he said weakly.

"Really, I'm sorry," she replied. "I was just going to ask you if you would open this window."

"I fancy it's malaria," he added. His teeth chattered slightly, as much from fright as from a desire to back up his statement.

"I've got some brandy in my case, if you'll kindly reach it down for me," said the woman.

"Not for the world . . . I mean, I never take anything for malaria," he said quickly.

"I suppose you caught it in the tropics?"

Theodoric knew nothing at all about the tropics. He felt that even the malaria tale was slipping from him. Would it be possible, he wondered, to explain the real story to her in small bits?

"Are you afraid of mice?" he asked carefully. He was growing, if possible, even more red in the face.

"Not unless there are an awful lot of them. Why do you ask?"

"I had one crawling inside my clothes just now," said Theodoric. His voice hardly seemed his own. "It was a most awkward situation."

"It must have been, if you wear your clothes at all tight," she said. "But mice like small, dark places."

"I had to get rid of it while you were asleep," he continued. Then, with a gulp, he added, "It was getting rid of it that brought me to . . . to this."

"Surely getting rid of one small mouse wouldn't bring on a chill," she exclaimed.

Theodoric was sure he heard a laugh in her voice.

It seemed she had guessed something of his problem. Was she enjoying his confusion? All the blood in his body seemed to rush to his face. The pain of his hurt pride was worse than a thousand mice. And then, as he thought about it, fear began to take the place of embarrassment. With every minute that passed, the train was rushing nearer to the crowded station. There, dozens of eyes would take the place of the one pair that watched him from the corner of the train car.

He had only one hope. Maybe in the next few minutes the young lady would go back to sleep. But as the minutes ticked by, that hope faded away. He peeked at her from time to time. She was wide awake.

"I think we must be getting near the station now," she said after a moment.

With growing fear Theodoric had already noticed the small, ugly houses they now passed. These marked the outskirts of the town and the journey's end. Her words seemed to be a signal. Suddenly he moved like a hunted animal breaking cover and dashing madly towards some other hiding place. Throwing aside the blanket, he fought his way back into his wrinkled clothing.

Out of the corner of his eye, he saw more buildings race past the window. He sensed a choking, hammering feeling in his throat and heart. And he was aware of a cold silence in that corner towards which he could not look. At last he sank back in his seat, clothed and dizzy. The train slowed down to a final crawl. The woman spoke.

"Would you be so kind," she asked, "as to get me a cab? I'm sorry to trouble you when you're feeling unwell. But being blind makes one so helpless at a train station."

Thinking About
the Stories

Sredni Vashtar

1. An author builds the plot around the conflict in a story. In this story, what forces or characters are struggling against each other? How is the conflict finally resolved?

2. Which character in this story do you most admire? Why? Which character do you like the least?

3. Suppose this story had a completely different outcome. Can you think of another effective ending for this story?

The Open Window

1. Interesting story plots often have unexpected twists and turns. What surprises did you find in this story?

2. Compare and contrast at least two characters in this story. In what ways are they alike? In what ways are they different?

3. Imagine that you have been asked to write a short review of this story. In one or two sentences, tell what the story is about and why someone would enjoy reading it.

Tobermory

1. What is the title of this story? Can you think of another good title?

2. How long ago was this story written? Think about the readers of that time. How were their lives different from the lives of today's readers? Was their purpose for reading the same or different? Were their tastes in reading the same or different? In what ways?

3. Who is the main character in this story? Who are one or two of the minor characters? Describe each of these characters in one or two sentences.

Dusk

1. Good writing always has an effect on the reader. How did you feel when you finished reading this story? Were you surprised, horrified, amused, sad, touched, or inspired? What elements in the story made you feel that way?

2. How important is the background of the story? Is weather a factor in the story? Is there a war going on or some other unusual circumstance? What influence does the background have on the characters' lives?

3. Did the story plot change direction at any point? Explain the turning point of the story.

The Mouse

1. All stories fit into one or more categories. Is this story serious or funny? Would you call it an adventure, a love story, or a mystery? Is it a character study? Or is it simply a picture the author has painted of a certain time and place? Explain your thinking.

2. Where does this story take place? Is there anything unusual about it? What effect does the place have on the characters?

3. Does the main character in this story have an internal conflict? Does a terrible decision have to be made? Explain the character's choices.

Thinking About
the Book

1. Choose your favorite illustration in this book. Use this picture as a springboard to write a new story. Give the characters different names. Begin your story with something they are saying or thinking.

2. Compare the stories in this book. Which was the most interesting? Why? In what ways were they alike? In what ways different?

3. Good writers usually write about what they know best. If you wrote a story, what kind of characters would you create? What would be the setting?